# Monkey: Not ready for Kindergarten

## Marc Brown

Alfred A. Knopf · New York

What if his teacher doesn't like him?

What if he gets on the wrong bus?

What if he can't find the bathroom?

What if they have peas for snacks?

What if they don't have red crayons?

What if he can't remember the whole alphabet?

What if he doesn't make new friends?

Why does Monkey need to go to kindergarten anyway?

He can already count to 12, and he usually remembers most of the alphabet.

He gets a backpack and some new sneakers with orange laces.

But he's still not ready.

When it's his brother's turn to be the teacher, he tells Monkey about show-and-tell and MUSIC class.

He teaches Monkey about using Inside Voices.

At the library, Monkey and his parents read all the books about kindergarten.

The night before Kindergarten, Monkey helps make his lunch.

He tucks his favorite book about bugs deep down into his backpack. Something to remind him of home.

He counts to twelve in the bathtub.

He falls asleep practicing the alphabet.

And then it's the **Big Day.**

Mommy and Daddy give Monkey hugs and kisses.

And he gives them the secret goodbye handshake they practiced.

For
·Bonnie Brown Walmsley·

THIS IS A BORZOI BOOK PUBLISHED BY ALFRED A. KNOPF

Copyright © 2015 by Marc Brown

All rights reserved. Published in the United States by Alfred A. Knopf,
an imprint of Random House Children's Books, a division of Random House LLC,
a Penguin Random House Company, New York.

Knopf, Borzoi Books, and the colophon are registered trademarks
of Random House LLC.

Visit us on the Web! randomhousekids.com

Educators and librarians, for a variety of teaching tools,
visit us at RHTeachersLibrarians.com

Library of Congress Cataloging-in-Publication Data
Brown, Marc Tolon, author, illustrator.
  Monkey : not ready for kindergarten / by Marc Brown. — First edition.
     pages   cm.
Summary: Kindergarten is just a week away and Monkey is not ready, but with help
and encouragement from family and friends, he begins to get excited.
ISBN 978-0-553-49658-1 (trade) — ISBN 978-0-553-49659-8 (lib. bdg.) —
ISBN 978-0-553-49660-4 (ebook)
[1. First day of school—Fiction. 2. Kindergarten—Fiction.
3. Monkeys—Fiction.] I. Title.
PZ7.B81618Mk 2015
[E]—dc23
2014002818

The text of this book was created by hand by Marc Brown, accompanied by
a few typeset bits set in Elephant.
The illustrations were created using colored pencils and gouache.

MANUFACTURED IN CHINA
July 2015
10 9 8 7 6 5 4 3 2 1
First Edition